jazz age
josephine

by Jonah Winter

illustrated by
marjorie Priceman

ATHENEUM BOOKS FOR YOUNG READERS
New York London Toronto Sydney New Delhi

People, listen to my story, 'bout a girl named Josephine.
People, listen to this story, 'bout a poor girl name of Josephine.

She was the saddest little sweetheart
this side of New Orleans.

Well, she was born up in St. Louis,
and she grew up with those St. Louis blues.

Yes, she was born in old St. Louis,
and she grew up singin' nothin' but the blues.

She just had one old ragged dress
and a pair of worn-out old shoes.

You see, the shack where she lived,
it didn't have no heat.
Things were sometimes so bad,
there wasn't **nothin'** to eat.

She slept down on the floor,
newspapers for a sheet—
rats crawlin' all around,
a-nibblin' at her feet.

"Josephine," her grandma said,
"I got a fairy tale for you.

Josephine, oh Josephine,
this story's 'bout a girl like you.

Someday you're gonna be a princess—
you know **what Granny says is true.**"

That's so hard to believe in, when the kids all act so cruel.
To believe in fairy tales . . . is so hard when folks are cruel.

Ain't nothin' left to do
but just pretend to be a fool.

So Josephine made funny faces,
     stuck out her tongue, and crossed her eyes.
Yes, Josephine made funny faces,
     stuck out her tongue, bugged out her eyes—
strutted right into a dance tent
     and then to everyone's surprise . . .

she did the Grizzly Bear

and she did the
Turkey Trot.

She whipped right through
the Bunny Hug,

strutted through the
Camel Walk.

She did so many dance steps
it made the people holler.
And when the dance was over,
Josephine got paid a dollar.

She kept dancin',

she kept dancin' . . .

and she never ever got tired.

She kept dancin',

she kept dancin' . . .

that girl, she never got tired. . . .

Until one night when her whole world changed:
the night St. Louis caught on fire.

Well, there were white folks chasin' black folks—
on the black folks' side of town . . .

white folks screamin' at the black folks . . .
and settin' fire to their town.

And the black folks kept on runnin'
while their homes burned to the ground.

So Josephine,
she started runnin' too,
she started runnin' on that night.

Yes, she started runnin',
runnin', runnin',
runnin',

RUNNIN'—started runnin' on that night.

There had to be some better place
where white folks treat you right.

She ran all around the country
with an old-time travelin' show.
Yes, she ran all around the USA
with an outdoor travelin' show,
doin' all her crazy dance steps
till it was time to pack up and go.

But the blues ran right behind her,
all the way to Old New York.
Them nasty blues ran right behind her,
till the world was cold and dark.
She didn't have no friends or money—
slept on a bench in Central Park.

She auditioned for this big show.
They told her, "Beat it, kid."
So she went out in the alley,
bawled her eyes out, flipped her lid.

The director, he took pity,
called her name out, had a heart.
He put her in the chorus line—
that's how she got her start.

Josephine, oh Josephine, you know you're in the big time now.

Josephine, oh Josephine,
grown up and in the big time now,
makin' people hoot and whistle
every night you take your bow.

Well, she wore big baggy pants,
she wore black makeup on her face.
Each night she wore these baggy pants,
she wore what people called "blackface."

As much as all those white folks loved her,
it was an insult to her race.

That was IT for Josephine.
She had made up her mind.
She'd stop clownin' for these folks

and leave those bllluuuuues behind.

So she jumped on a boat
...as headed for France.
...ne was gonna show those French folks

how Americans dance.

It was the Jazz Age now,
year of 1925:
jumpin' jazz bands, sassy haircuts—
yes, the good times
had arrived!

Miss Liberty waved bye-bye
as the boat sailed out to sea,
and for the first time in her life
Jazz Age Josephine felt free!

Then . . .

[One, two, three—HIT IT!]

Gay Paree!
Josephine!
Here's an act
they've *never* seen!

(Boh doh doh-dee-oh!)

Paris, France—
instant fame!
Everybody
knows her name!

Boh doh doh-dee-oh
Boh doh doh-dee-oh
Dohhhhhhhhhhhhhhh . . . !

Boodle-am boodle-am boodle-am SHAKE!
Boodle-am boodle-am boodle-am SHAKE!

Zee-buh-dop zoo-buh-dop zee-buh-dop ZOW!
Zop zop zop zop zoo-buh-dop ZOW!

Panther, camel—
who's that, who?

Ostrich, parakeet—kangaroo?

Can she dance?
That's a fact!
Belly to belly and
back to back!

It's the Shake,

the Shimmy,

and the Mess Around!

No one sleeps
when she's in town!

Can she sing?
You'd sing too
if everything you'd ever dreamed of . . .
suddenly *just happened*
like a beautiful song. . . .

How wonderful to be adored
like a princess,
like a queen,
and to glitter like a diamond—
just the thrill of being seen
and known and loved by everyone you pass.

How wonderful to be a star,
to live in a palace,
to keep a goat and a tiger
and a monkey as pets!
To walk a cheetah named Chiquita
through the boulevards of Paris,
        and yet—alas!—

to long for the place
where you were born,
where you would never live again,
imagining how it might have been
not to be scorned for the color of your skin,
not to be forced to run away, and yet . . .

DrumBEATS.
    Bright LIGHTS.

Josephine is the
    STAR TONIGHT:

Dressed to the hilt, she is
singin' a lilt about
Pretty Little Baby that'll Alabama-lama-wham-ya—

Bye-BYE,
BlackBIRD. She ain't
singin' the blues, she's got
nothin' to lose:

Show after show, she is makin' a go of it, dancin' the Charleston, beggin' your pardon, ma'am, nanners and feathers and glitterin' diamonds and here comes the end of this jazz fairy tale about—

AUTHOR'S NOTE

JOSEPHINE BAKER was born Freda Josephine McDonald on June 3, 1906 in St. Louis, Missouri. As a girl, her natural entertaining abilities did indeed provide a ticket out of the poverty, racism, and general misery of her childhood. And Josephine was, in fact, still a girl when she got her first big break into the world of New York show business. She was fifteen years old, to be exact, and she lied about her age to get into the show, "Shuffle Along." So talented was she in her clowning role in this show, as it turned out, that Baker quickly became the highest paid Broadway showgirl of her era. Her popularity in New York, though, was nothing compared to the immediate rise to fame she experienced in Paris upon her arrival in 1925, at the tender age of nineteen years old. Baker's French audiences embraced her with an enthusiasm she would never experience in her homeland, where she had been offered only humiliating roles. For Parisians, though, she became an exotic, beloved symbol of the American Jazz Age, in full swing during the 1920s.

As her performing days were tapering off, Josephine adopted twelve children from around the world and called them the "Rainbow Tribe." Her commitment to racial integration did not stop here. In 1963, she spoke at the same civil rights convention in Washington, D.C., where the Reverend Martin Luther King, Jr. made his famous speech, "I Have a Dream." Josephine Baker died on April 12, 1975. During her funeral procession through Paris, more than 20,000 mourners lined the streets.

For my very own Jazz Age Sally
—J. W.

To Mom and Dad
—M. P.

ATHENEUM BOOKS FOR YOUNG READERS • An imprint of Simon & Schuster Children's Publishing Division • 1230 Avenue of the Americas, New York, New York 10020 • Text copyright © 2012 by Jonah Winter • Illustrations copyright © 2012 by Marjorie Priceman • All rights reserved, including the right of reproduction in whole or in part in any form. • ATHENEUM BOOKS FOR YOUNG READERS is a registered trademark of Simon & Schuster, Inc. • For information about special discounts for bulk purchases, please contact Simon & Schuster Special Sales at 1-866-506-1949 or business@simonandschuster.com. • The Simon & Schuster Speakers Bureau can bring authors to your live event. For more information or to book an event, contact the Simon & Schuster Speakers Bureau at 1-866-248-3049 or visit our website at www.simonspeakers.com. • Book design by Debra Sfetsios-Conover • The text for this book is set in Parisian. • The illustrations for this book are rendered in gouache and ink. • Manufactured in China • 0512 SCP • 10 9 8 7 6 5 4 3 2 • CIP data for this book is available from the Library of Congress. • ISBN 978-1-4169-6123-9 • ISBN 978-1-4424-4710-3 (eBook)